My FIRST BOOK of NATURE

The Seashore

Victoria Munson

WINDMILL BOOKS

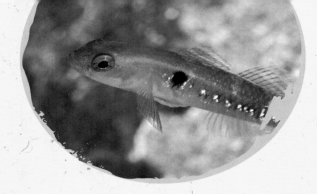

Published in 2019 by Windmill Books,
an Imprint of Rosen Publishing
29 East 21st Street, New York, NY 10010

Editor: Victoria Brooker
Book Design: Elaine Wilkinson

Photo Credits:
Istock: 5b zoerae28; 6 milynmiles; 21t Rex_
Wholster; Shutterstock: cover main David
Osborn; (bl) Nicolas Primola; (tl) Raymond
Llewellyn; (br) Bjoern Buxbaum Conradi; (tr)
Peter Moulton; (mr) Tamara Kulikova; 2t, 17
Joao Pedro Silva; 2b, 11 lobster20; 3t, 13
Emi; 3b Lorna Munden; 4 Triple H Images; 5t
DJTTaylor; 7t Aleksey Stemmer, 7b lauraslens;
8Paul Nash; 9t Ruud Morijn Photographer; 9b
Johnson76; 10 Zharate; 11t Martin Fowler;
11b lobster20; 12 Arto Hakola; 13t Florian
Andronache; 13b V. Belov; 14 CHAINFOTO24;
14b Marsha Mood; 15t Janet S; 15b Jausa; 16
MP cz; 17t Seaphotoart; 17b Aries Sutanto; 18t
Tory Kalliman; 18b Willyam Bradberry; 19t David
Osborn; 19b Andrew M. Allport; 20 Becky Stares;
21b C Tatiana; Naturepl

Cataloging-in-Publication Data

Names: Munson, Victoria.
Title: The Seashore / Victoria Munson.
Description: New York : Windmill Books, 2019. |
Series: My first book of nature | Includes glossary
and index.
Identifiers: LCCN ISBN 9781508196204 (pbk.)
| ISBN 9781508196198 (library bound) | ISBN
9781508196211 (6 pack)
Subjects: LCSH: Seashore--Juvenile literature. |
Seashore ecology--Juvenile literature. | Seashore
biology--Juvenile literature.
Classification: LCC QH95.7 M86 2019 | DDC
578.769'9--dc23

Manufactured in the United States of America

CPSIA Compliance Information: Batch #BS18WM:
For Further Information contact Rosen Publishing,
New York, New York at 1-800-237-9932

Contents

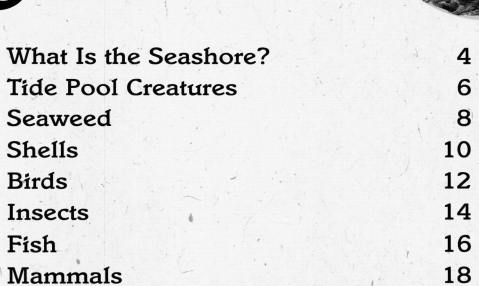

What Is the Seashore?

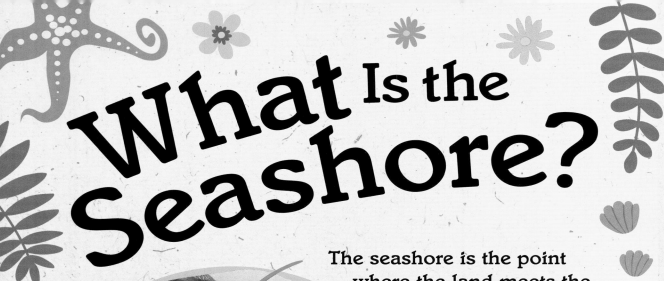

The seashore is the point where the land meets the sea. Seashores can be sandy, rocky, or pebbly.

Seashores are home to many different plants and animals.

Twice a day, the sea moves up the shore and back down again. These movements are called tides. At high tide, waves are at the top part of the beach. Low tide is when the sea is at the lowest part of the beach.

Some beaches have tide pools. Fish hide when a shadow covers their tide pool.

Animals such as anemones and crabs live in tide pools.

Many sea animals stay in the same place, so it is easy to spot them.

Tide times are different every day. Check the tide times before you go to the seashore.

The best time to look for nature on the beach is when the tide is out.

Tide Pool Creatures

Acorn barnacles have gray-white shells with a diamond-shaped opening at the top. When the tide is out, the shell will be closed.

When underwater, the barnacles open and stick out feathery limbs.

Barnacles attach themselves to rocks and never move again.

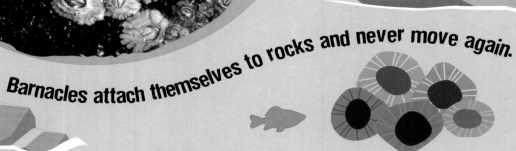

Shore crabs are a brownish-green color. All crabs have four pairs of legs and a front pair of pincers. Pincers are used to fight and catch prey.

Female crabs can lay up to **185,000** eggs at a time.

Shore crabs eat barnacles and dog whelks.

Purple sea stars live in the Pacific Ocean. They eat other tide pool creatures, such as barnacles and snails.

Sea stars have suckers to hold onto rocks.

Sea stars are also called starfish.

Seaweed

Rockweed sticks to rocks using a "holdfast," which is a round, root-like growth.

Rockweed air bladders are egg shaped.

You can estimate the age of rockweed by counting the bladders, because one bladder grows each year.

Bladderwrack gets its name from its rounded air bladders.

These air bladders help the seaweed to **float** in the sea.

Bladderwrack is used for food and medicine.

Sea lettuce clings to rocks using a holdfast. It looks crumpled and reminds people of lettuce leaves.

Sea lettuce can be cooked and eaten. It is full of vitamins and minerals.

Shells

Shells are homes for soft-bodied creatures called mollusks.

Limpets have gray-white cone-shaped shells.

When the tide is in, limpets move around on rocks. As the tide goes out, they return to the same spot by following the mucus trail they left behind.

There is sometimes a dent in the rock where limpets have been because they return to the same spot so often.

Dog whelks usually have creamy-yellowish or light-gray shells. They can also be orange, yellow, brown, or black.

Dog whelks were used in medieval times to produce purple dyes.

Dog whelks make holes in limpet shells and suck out the flesh inside.

Cockles have creamy-brown ridged shells.

Cockles are eaten by humans, fish, and birds.

Birds

Black-headed gulls get their name from their black head. However, it is only black in summer.

For the rest of the year, black-headed gulls have a white head with chocolate-brown stripes.

Herring gulls have a hooked yellow bill with a red spot.

Herring gulls are **large,**

NOISY BIRDS.

In winter, their head is streaked with gray-brown marks. For the rest of the year, their head is white.

Oystercatchers have black and white bodies with a long, bright orange beak.

Oystercatchers will sometimes lay their eggs in a gull's nest.

Oystercatchers use their long beak to break open limpet shells to eat them.

Insects

Monarch butterflies have reddish-orange wings with black patterns.

The red-orange color warns other animals not to eat them.

They are most active at night, but can sometimes be seen in the daytime, too.

Monarch butterfly caterpillars are also brightly colored, with black, white, and yellow stripes.

Swallowtail butterflies can be found on flowers near sandy beaches.

The eastern tiger swallowtail has yellow wings with blue markings at the bottom.

Sand digger wasps have a black body with a bright orange waist.

They sting caterpillars and then drag them back to their nest.

The wasps lay their eggs inside the caterpillars' bodies. When the wasp eggs hatch, the newborn larvae eat the caterpillars.

Fish

Rock gobies are covered in dark brown blotches that make them hard to spot.

Gobies lay up to **7,000 eggs** at one time.

Gobies have suckers on fins underneath their bodies. These suckers help them stick to rocks so that they aren't washed away.

Tompot blenny fish have big round eyes, a large head, and a thin body.

They are orangey brown, with dark brown lines.

Tompot blennies have feathery tentacles on top of their head.

Pufferfish inflate to scare away predators. They are also very poisonous.

Pufferfish live all over the world.

Mammals

Bottlenose dolphins are gray with a long bottle-shaped beak.

Bottlenose dolphins like to follow boats and can be seen leaping out of the water beside them.

Dolphins have a blowhole on the top of their head through which they get air.

A group of dolphins is called a pod.

Gray seals live on the coasts of the North Atlantic Ocean.

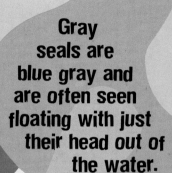

Gray seals are blue gray and are often seen floating with just their head out of the water.

Gray seal pups have white fur when they are born.

Common seals have a rounded face. They are brown or gray with dark spots.

In water, common seals can reach speeds of 18 mph (30 km/h).

Plants

Marram grass is the tall and spiky grass that grows in and around sand dunes.

Its glossy thin leaves are rolled up to hold in water.

Marram grass has long roots to help it find water. The roots also hold the sand in the dunes together to stop them from being blown away.

Yellow-horned poppies have bright yellow petals. The leaves are thick and rough.

Sap from yellow-horned poppies' stems is very poisonous.

Yellow-horned poppies get their name from their seed pods, which are long and curved like elephants' tusks.

Thrift has round, pink flower heads. It has tall hairy stems. Thrift leaves are tightly packed together, forming a cushion on the ground.

Thrift is also known as sea pink, ladies' cushion, and Mary's pillow.

Seashore Shells

At the seashore, see what empty shells you can find.

1

Periwinkles
Periwinkles have a thick, rounded shell with gray-brown spirals. Sometimes they have a sharp point on the end, although the point eventually gets worn away by the sea.

2

Limpets
Limpets are gray-white cone-shaped shells. Limpets higher up the shore will have taller shells than those found on the lower shore.

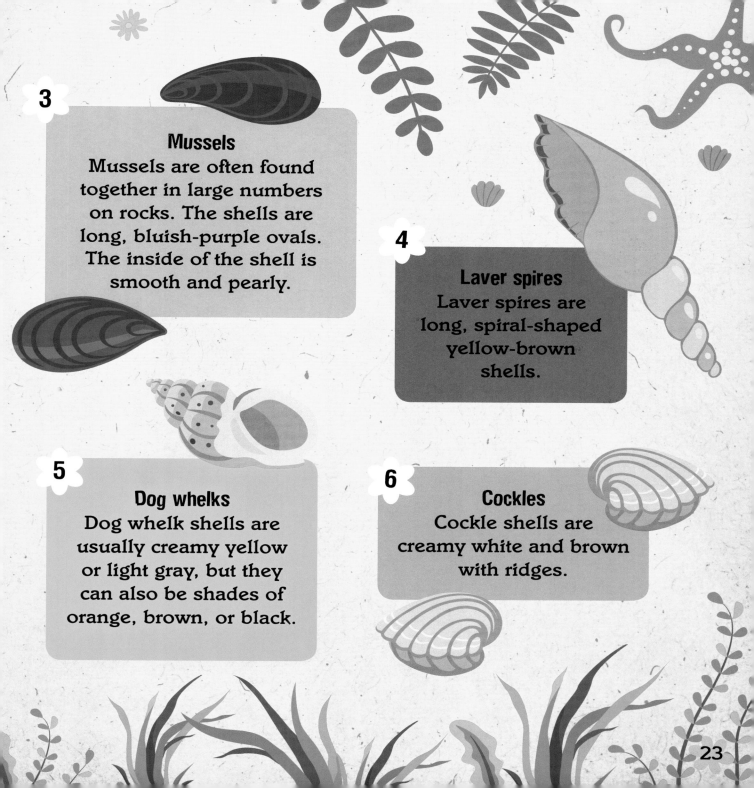

Mussels
Mussels are often found together in large numbers on rocks. The shells are long, bluish-purple ovals. The inside of the shell is smooth and pearly.

3

Laver spires
Laver spires are long, spiral-shaped yellow-brown shells.

4

Dog whelks
Dog whelk shells are usually creamy yellow or light gray, but they can also be shades of orange, brown, or black.

5

Cockles
Cockle shells are creamy white and brown with ridges.

6

Glossary and Index

larvae the young worm-like stage in an insect's life cycle

suckers part of an animal's body used for attaching to things

tentacles flexible arms of an animal used for grabbing things and moving